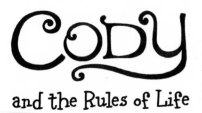

Cody

and the Rules of Life

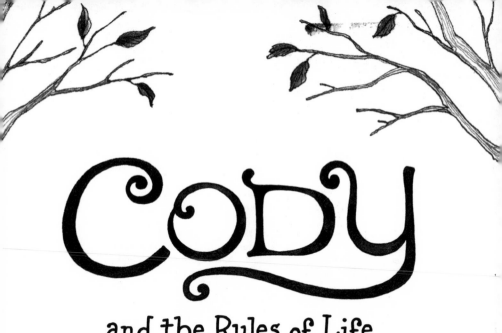

CODY

and the Rules of Life

TRICIA SPRINGSTUBB

illustrated by
ELIZA WHEELER

CANDLEWICK PRESS

Text copyright © 2017 by Tricia Springstubb
Illustrations copyright © 2017 by Eliza Wheeler

First edition 2017

Library of Congress Catalog Card Number pending
ISBN 978-0-7636-7920-0

17 18 19 20 21 22 BVG 10 9 8 7 6 5 4 3 2 1

Printed in Berryville, VA, U.S.A.

This book was typeset in Dante.
The illustrations were done in ink and watercolor.

Candlewick Press
99 Dover Street
Somerville, Massachusetts 02144

visit us at www.candlewick.com

For Phoebe, who always thinks for herself
T. S.

For Renee: best biology lab partner ever
and always a true-blue friend
E. W.

1
The Cobra

In this life, many things are hard to predict:

Hiccups

Balloons

Big brothers

This afternoon, Cody's big brother was staring at his laptop. His eyes bulged. His jaw flapped. Looking at him, you would never guess Wyatt was a genius. To tell the truth, he looked kind of insane.

"Man!" Wyatt said. "Rear shocks with boost valve technology!"

Cody hoped he was finally going to build a robot. One that would do all the chores, so that when Mom came home from work she could put her feet up and drink her fizzy water in peace. It would be nice if the robot could also write spelling sentences. And pop out a plain pizza, extra cheese, any time you said *"Azzip!"* which is *Pizza!* backward.

But when she leaned over her brother's shoulder, all Cody saw was a bike.

"Sweet!" Wyatt said. "Adjustable compression. Crank set with bash guard and WT-six-sixty-six wheels."

"You already have a bike," Cody said.

"That's a kid bike." Wyatt wiggled his shoulders as if Cody were an annoying itch, instead of his beloved sister. "I need a *vehicle.*"

"Your bike has those cool Mario stickers on it." Cody leaned in closer.

"I rest my case."

Cody leaned in even closer and, oops, somehow she toppled onto Wyatt, who bumped his water bottle, which tipped onto the keyboard . . .

Fast forward, please.

Outside, Cody paid a visit to her pet ants. Winter was upon them, and the ants were hibernating. Not a single one in sight. Cody gave a sigh. Winter was a hard time for a bug-lover.

When Dad got home, Wyatt showed him the new bike, which was called the Cobra. He pointed out the many special, deluxe features. For a minute, Dad looked like he was falling into a bike trance, too. Then he scratched his head.

"That's a pile of dough, Wy. You sure you want to spend all your hard-earned money?"

"A robot would be more useful," Cody added.

Wyatt paid no attention to her.

"I'm sure, Dad," he said. "Two hundred percent sure."

"It's a fine bike," said Dad. "And you're a responsible guy. I trust you to exercise your judgment."

Dad never said he trusted Cody's judgment. Which who knew what that was, and why it needed exercise.

"Is that a yes?" asked Wyatt.

Wyatt looked at Dad. Dad looked at Wyatt. It was a man-to-man moment.

At last, Dad nodded.

"Yes!" Wyatt punched the air. "This is the best day of my life!"

He and Dad got busy ordering the Cobra. Dad said he'd pay the extra money for quick delivery. They both ignored Cody. She had to check to make sure she had not gone invisible.

At times like this, what Cody needed was Gremlin.

Gremlin used to belong to Wyatt. The day her brother gave Gremlin to her, she thought she was dreaming. Wyatt adored that rubber monster! Cody wasn't even allowed to breathe on Gremlin. But that day, Wyatt announced he was too old for toys. He handed Gremlin to her and, quick-quick, walked away.

Gremlin looked fierce, but underneath he had a heart of gold. He was an excellent listener, and he agreed with everything Cody said.

"What's so great about brand-new?" she asked him. "You're not new, but you're still the best."

Gremlin gazed back with eyes of I-totally-agree.

Cody tucked him into his special cave of pillows. Gremlin was brave, but sometimes he got scared of the dark. Cody had to take him out and comfort him.

Now Gremlin waved his claws. This was monster for "I love you, too."

2
The Rookie

Cody's teacher, Mr. Daniels, started every day with his shirt tucked in and his hair combed. By lunchtime, his shirt hung out and a piece of hair at the back of his head stuck straight up like a little flagpole.

It was fascinating.

Pearl, Cody's best school friend, said Mr. Daniels was a rookie. This was a fun word to say, and meant they were the first class he ever taught.

On his desk, Mr. Daniels kept a small, beautiful gong. When he tapped it with the little hammer, it made a peaceful, hushed sound, like a bell wearing fuzzy slippers. If you stood close enough, you could feel it gong-ing inside you. Cody stood close as often as possible.

Mr. Daniels had rules for everything. Some were just regular rules, like Indoor Voices. But some were

what he called Non-Negotiable. That meant *No exceptions ever no matter what till the end of time.*

Only Mr. Daniels was allowed to gong. That was N-N.

He did it now. *Gongggg.*

"Journal Time!" he said. "Today's topic is Something I Am Thankful For."

Cody heaved a sigh. She liked to read, but not to write. *Blah, blah, blah,* that's how Journal Time felt.

At their table, Gopal was listing every computer game ever invented. Madison drew pictures of her many cousins. Pearl just sat there with her eyes closed, tapping her pencil on her chin.

This was strange. Pearl was good at everything. She could make super-complicated origami. She was such a great piano player, she'd win *Top Talent* if she ever went on. Not to mention, Pearl was pretty as a princess.

You might think that Pearl was a pain in the neck, but you would be wrong. Pearl was a friend to all, and especially to Cody.

"Are you okay?" Cody asked.

"I'm thinking." Pearl did not open her eyes. "I

don't want to go on automatic pilot. I want to write something deep and meaningful."

This was a new and interesting idea. Cody decided to try it. She closed her eyes, too.

A conveyor belt appeared. The people and things she loved went slowly by. Suddenly, the conveyor belt stopped. A spotlight beamed down on one thing.

Cody's eyes flew open. She grabbed her pencil. She wrote:

I am thankful for Gremlin. He used to belong to my brother, Wyatt. He is green with bumpy skin. Gremlin not Wyatt.

Cody paused. She tapped her pencil on her chin. Then she added:

Wyatt gave Gremlin to me. I am never giving him to anyone.

That last sentence didn't sound so thankful. But it was true.

Besides, all Wyatt cares about is his cobra.

Cody tipped her chair back on two legs. Writing something deep and meaningful was different from writing the same old thing. It was like the difference between eating freeze-dried astronaut ice cream or the real, creamy thing. No comparison.

"Four on the Floor, Cody!" called Mr. Daniels. "Important class rule!"

Cody set her chair down flat. Pearl was busy writing now. Side by side, she and Cody wrote deep, meaningful things. Cody was so glad they were friends.

At lunch recess, Cody played with Pearl and Spencer. They raced around being fiery dragons, huffing and puffing steam clouds. Until . . .

"Avast!" Molly Meen pointed her invisible pirate sword at Spencer. "Prepare to be shark bait, lad!"

Pearl stepped in front of Spencer to protect him. She narrowed her eyes.

"Molly Meen, where did you get that scarf? It looks exactly like Sophie's new one."

"Aaargh!" growled the Pirate Queen. "The lass gave it to me!"

This was Molly Meen for "I snatched it from her and what are you going to do about it?"

"Shiver me timbers!" yelled Molly as she ran away.

"I don't like her," Spencer said.

"I don't like her *behavior*," Pearl said.

In this life, some things are what you call total opposites:

Summer and winter

Marshmallows and spinach

Pearl and Molly Meen

That night, Wyatt came home with a new bike helmet. And a special water bottle called a Hydration System. He also had something called toe clips, which did not sound pleasant, in Cody's opinion. Who knew riding a bike could get so complicated?

"Want to play hide-and-seek with me and Gremlin?" Cody asked him.

"Look at this clip's quick-release action," Wyatt said.

Her brother had started speaking another language. The language of bike.

3
Sproing!

When Cody got her journal back the next day, it had a note from Mr. Daniels:

Very good writing! I'd like to meet Gremlin and Wyatt. I'm not so sure about the cobra.

"Hooray!" said Pearl. "You got a sticker. Can I read it?"

They traded journals. Pearl's said:

I am thankful for my endangered-animal collection. My grandmother sends me one for every special occasion. They come with adoption certificates. When I look at them, I think of my beautiful, loving grandmother.

Aw! That was so nice. And look—Pearl had gotten the same frog sticker.

"We're twins," said Pearl.

Before she knew it, Cody was leapfrogging around, making Gopal laugh so hard he tipped his chair back and . . .

Fast forward, please.

"Are you okay?" Mr. Daniels helped Gopal up from the floor.

"Yup," said Gopal. "My mother says I have a really hard head."

"Class, there is a reason we have rules like Four on the Floor." Mr. Daniels looked stern. "Rules keep us safe. They help us get our work done. They keep things fair and square."

He ran a hand over his hair but, *sproing!* It popped back up.

If you asked Cody, fair and square would be Mr.
Daniels sharing his gong.

But in this life, teachers do not usually ask your
opinion.

Just before they went home,
Pearl handed Cody an origami
frog.

"Unfold it," she said.

Inside, in Pearl's neat-as-a-
pin handwriting, it said:

Please come
for a
sleepover
on
Saturday

Cody had always wanted to go on a sleepover. Once, Spencer had stayed overnight, but that didn't count because it was really babysitting, plus he was homesick the whole time.

"This will be my first official sleepover," Pearl said.

"Me too!" Cody said. "We're twins again."

"My baby brothers are twins," said Pearl. "I always wished I had a twin of my own!"

Together, they did some careful, no-rule-breaking, twin-frog hopping.

When Cody got home, Wyatt's bike had been delivered. ASSEMBLY REQUIRED, said the box. He was studying the instructions.

"I'll help you put it together," said Cody.

Wyatt glanced around the garage, like by a miracle someone else would appear.

"Okay," he said. "But don't touch anything unless I say."

Cody had never helped build something for real before. Little by little, she and Wyatt fitted those pieces together till, ta-da! The separate parts turned into one whole, complete thing. A sleek, shiny bike that said COBRA on the side.

Wyatt gazed at it the same goofy way he looked at Payton Underwood, the girl of his dreams. If that bike were a girl, Wyatt would ask it to marry him.

"Tell *la madre* I went for a test ride." Wyatt snapped his new helmet on. "Tell her I'll be careful, et cetera, et cetera."

Zoom! He and the Cobra left Cody in the dust.

She checked the ants. No activity. She squinted at the sky. Gray clouds. Wyatt's old, abandoned bike leaned in the corner of the garage. Cody gave it a cheer-up pat. When her big brother still didn't come home, she schlumped inside.

Mom was looking up recipes. It was her day off from her job as Head of Shoes at O'Becker Department Store, but she wore her gold hoop earrings and pretend-alligator boots. Mom never took a day off from being stylish.

"How about turnip-parsnip crumble?" she said.

Cody put her hands around her throat. She

fell to the floor and pretended to die from parsnip poisoning.

"Well, how about stewed tomatoes with oatmeal?"

Cooking was not high on Mom's list of talents. Sitting under the table, Cody watched her cross and uncross her pretend-alligator ankles.

"Pearl invited me to sleep over," Cody said.

Mom's head appeared under the table. "That's nice," she said with an upside-down smile. "Do you want to go?"

"Do bears poop in the woods?" Wyatt had taught Cody this useful phrase.

"You've never had a sleepover," said Mom. "It might feel a little strange."

Cody thought this over. "I'll bring Gremlin," she said.

"You are so smart. Between you and me, I bet Wyatt couldn't have put that bike together without you."

"He didn't even say thank you."

"That's too bad. I'm sure he *felt* thankful."

"Ha." Cody's eyes suddenly felt hot. It got hard to swallow. "All he cares about is that bike. He loves it better than anything in the whole world."

Now Mom came to sit under the table, too. She took Cody's hands in hers.

"That's impossible. A boy can't love anything, even the world's best bike, more than his sister. You know why?"

"Why?"

"Because a bike can't love him back."

Cody knew Mom was just trying to cheer her up. When mothers try to cheer kids up, they are not required to stick to the truth.

"Wyatt bought his own bike. You're having your first sleepover." Mom touched the tip of Cody's nose. "Just yesterday you were my tiny babies with dumpling cheeks and sausage legs."

"Mo-o-o-m!" said Cody, like a kid on TV who was dying of embarrassment.

Except she wasn't, not really. Secretly, Cody loved when Mom talked like that.

How Wyatt usually was at dinner: a silent eating machine.

How Wyatt was tonight: a world-champion blabbermouth.

"Eat your spaghetti," said Mom. In the history of Wyatt, nobody had ever had to say that to him before.

He couldn't stop talking about how the Cobra

handled on the icy road. How it practically got up to warp speed. How he rode over to Payton Underwood's house, and she said she'd never seen such a fabulous bike.

Payton! Wyatt was always trying to impress that silly girl.

"She couldn't believe I bought it with my own money and assembled it myself," he said.

"Didn't you tell P.U. I helped you?" Cody asked.

In this life, some questions are what you'd call a waste of time.

4
Double Heart Attack

The next morning, Cody was the first one up. She loved the early morning, when the whole day was waiting. Waiting for someone to push the START button.

Tonight was the sleepover. What should she do in the long meantime? Cody decided to check on the Cobra.

Clean Out Garage was always on Dad's chore list, because the minute he did, it filled right back up. He said the garage was like the geyser Old Faithful. Only instead of steam, the garage geysered up more junk.

The Cobra didn't look happy. It wasn't used to living with a dusty treadmill and old paint cans. Plus, Wyatt had locked it up with a heavy-duty lock. Anyone could see that bike was longing for some nice fresh air.

Cobra was the wrong name. If that bike were an animal, it wouldn't be a snake. It would be a horse. A horse named Midnight.

It belonged to her brother, Cody knew this very well. But if it weren't for her, it might not exist—even Mom had said so.

Wyatt kept the key hidden under a flowerpot. Cody undid the lock, then rolled Midnight/Cobra out onto the driveway.

If you are thinking this was easy, think again. Midnight/Cobra was much bigger and heavier than Cody's bike.

Plus, why did boy bikes have those dumb bars in the middle? Even on tiptoe, Cody couldn't get her leg over. A squirrel watched. *"Scritch, scritch,"* he scolded, and ran up the tree like he couldn't stand to watch.

Just as she was about to give up, she made it onto the seat.

Which was very skinny. No sooner did she plop her bungie on it than she began to slip back off. She gripped the handlebars. Her feet pedaled thin air.

Maybe this was not a good idea.

Uh-oh.

The bike was tilting sideways. In slow motion. The driveway was coming closer, closer . . .

Uh-oh, uh-oh!

Crunch!

OW!

She scrambled out from under the bike. Her knees and elbows hurt. Her heart was having a heart attack. What if she'd broken the bike? Using all her strength, she pushed it upright. The handlebars still steered. The wheels still spun.

But just when her heart was getting un-attacked, she noticed something. A teeny bit of paint had chipped off the *O* in *COBRA*. Now it looked more like a heart.

Maybe Wyatt wouldn't notice.

Anyway, the heart looked kind of nice, didn't it?

Uh-oh, uh-oh.

Quick-quick, Cody put that trouble-making bike back in the garage. *Click-click,* she re-locked the lock. When she tiptoed inside, everyone was still asleep.

Whew!

Cody pulled Gremlin out of his cave of pillows. Gremlin was indestructible. You could hug him as hard as you wanted and he didn't mind.

Plus, you could tell him any secret, and he would never blab.

• • •

Some days zoom by before you know it. Others last two zillion years. How can this be? In this life, time makes up its own rules.

After lunch, Cody went to see Spencer. He and his parents lived right around the corner with his grandmother. This was so nice.

The not-so-nice part was that the house was a side-by-side. And who should live on the other side but Molly Meen, Pirate Queen. She lived there with her little sister, Maxie. And their father, who killed bugs for a living.

Cody ran up the front steps. On weekends, Molly and Maxie stayed at their mother's house, so today the coast was clear. Inside, Spencer was practicing his violin. He played something called "Green Sleeves." A song about a shirt should have been silly, but Spencer made it serious and beautiful.

As he was putting his violin away, Cody said,

"Guess what? I'm sleeping over at Pearl's house tonight."

Spencer pushed his glasses up his nose. Even though he and Cody were such close friends they were practically related, they were not what you'd call two peas in a pod. For example, Spencer was anti-adventure. Just the word *sleepover* made him blink fast.

"You better bring your own pillow." *Blink-blink.* "In case Pearl's pillows are too fat or too flat or smell funny."

"Probably we'll stay up all night and won't even need pillows," Cody said.

"Humans require eight hours sleep," Spencer said. "It's a rule of good health."

"It's the weekend," said Cody. "Could we please not talk about rules?"

Spencer's grandmother GG made them cocoa with marshmallows. Marshmallows were one of Cody's top ten foods. GG kept them on hand just for her.

They sat on the porch swing with MewMew spread across their laps like a blanket that could purr. GG's side of the porch was the coziest spot on Earth, with wind chimes and tie-dyed cushions and pots just waiting for spring flowers. The Meen side had more in common with Cody's junk-geyser garage.

"Hey," said Cody. "Why is your remote-control car on the Meen side?"

"Oh." Spencer carefully sipped his cocoa. His glasses steamed up. "I guess I let Molly borrow it."

"Did you let her *borrow* your scooter, too?"

Spencer took another careful sip. Then another one. Suspicious, that's what Cody was getting, just as Wyatt rode up on the Cobra.

Inside Cody, alarm bells began to clang.

"Wow," said Spencer. "That is the coolest bike ever, in my experience."

Clang-clang! But Wyatt didn't glare at her with eyes of prepare-to-meet-your-doom-you-bike-wrecker-you. Instead, he smiled.

"You are right, *amiguito,*" he said.

He hadn't noticed the chipped paint. Just as the alarm bells faded away, Mr. Meen came out. He crossed the porch in his steel-toed, bug-exterminating boots.

"Yo, dude!" he said. "Killer machine!"

33

Wyatt pointed out the race-face bash guard and WT666 wheels. Cody could hardly breathe. Just as she was about to have the second heart attack of the day, Wyatt said he had to go.

"I don't want to expose the gears to the corrosive night air," he said.

Thank goodness for corrosive night air, whatever that was.

Mr. Meen watched Wyatt ride away. He folded his thick, muscle-y arms. He spoke softly, just to himself.

"Molly sure would dig a bike like that."

Molly was not what you'd call Cody's favorite person, but Cody had to smile. Mr. Meen was right. She could just see Molly tearing around on the Cobra, terrifying anybody who got in her way.

Mr. Meen rubbed his face. He scuffed his boot.

"You never know," he said to himself. "One of these days I might hit the lottery."

Stomp-stomp. Mr. Meen's big boots crossing the porch. *Whoosh-thunk.* The door closing behind him.

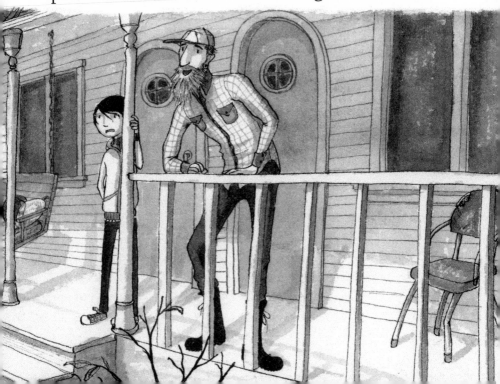

Cody collapsed onto the swing. What a day. She picked up her cocoa. By now the marshmallows were melted to goo.

"Did you already pack for the sleepover?" Spencer asked.

The sleepover! How could Cody have forgotten it? She jumped up.

"Remember to bring your own pillow!" Spencer called after her.

5
The Sleepover, Part 1

"Hello, Cody." Pearl held her front door open wide. "Welcome to the Official First-Ever Sleepover." She handed Cody an origami. "It's a pineapple. A symbol of welcome and hospitality."

"Wow," said Cody. It was all she could think to say, so she said it again. "Wow."

While Mom and Pearl's mother chatted, Pearl showed Cody around. Her house was neat and orderly, just like Pearl herself. Even her twin brothers, crawling around on the rug, had their baby hair neatly combed.

"Come say good-bye," called Mom.

She and Cody hugged.

"Have a wonderful time," Mom whispered in her ear. "And if you feel homesick, remember Gremlin."

After Mom left, Pearl's mother whisked a pizza out of the oven. Cody's stomach did a little flip. The pizza looked delicious. Also messy. What if she dripped tomato sauce in this spotless house?

"We can eat in the family room while we watch a movie," Pearl said. "Mom promised to keep the babies away from us."

The family room wasn't so neat. Cody began to feel right at home. She and Pearl sat on the couch, eating pizza and drinking chocolate milk. Cody had seen the movie before, but that was okay, because she and Pearl could sing along. At the best part, where the princess made red roses bloom out of the snow, Pearl jumped onto the couch. She threw her arms wide. Cody could practically see her tonsils, she sang so loud.

"Wow," said Cody.

"Want to know a secret?" Pearl asked when she got her breath back. "I'm going to have my own rock band. I'll play the keyboard and be the lead singer. All my clothes will sparkle, and my hair will be dyed purple."

This time, Cody could not even manage *wow.* Perfect, obedience-school Pearl wanted to be a rock singer?

"What do you want to be?" Pearl asked.

"A bug scientist." As soon as she said it, Cody felt bad. It sounded boring, compared to a rock star with sparkly outfits.

But Pearl nodded. "Insects are fascinating," she said.

"I know! If a flea were a human it could jump over a skyscraper. An ant can lift things that weigh a thousand times more than it does."

"Insects deserve more respect," said Pearl.

"I know! Most people think bugs are pests."

"I don't go by what most people think," said Pearl. "I think for myself."

Exactly like Pearl. That was how Cody wanted to be.

They ate more pizza and started another movie. Pearl's mother brought the babies in to say good night. They wore identical sleep suits that turned them into fuzzy little bundles.

"Pearl! Pearl!" they squealed. They were adorable. Not only that. They adored Pearl.

It crossed Cody's mind that a little brother might be better than a big one.

After movie number two, Cody and Pearl went to Pearl's room. Almost everything was purple. The walls, the rug, the sheets and quilt. It was like being inside a grape.

One thing was not purple: the animals lined up on the shelf over her bed. They were white as white can be.

"These are my endangered animals." Pearl swept her arm upward, like a lady on a game show. "So far I have all Arctic."

The Arctic Hare. The Arctic Fox. The Arctic Polar Bear. The Arctic Owl. The Arctic Baby Seal.

"Each one represents a real animal in the wild." Pearl showed Cody a folder. "These are their official adoption certificates. They cost a small fortune, but my grandmother says it's a worthy investment."

The animals were so clean. They looked untouched by human hands.

"Which is your favorite?" Cody asked.

"I can't pick," said Pearl. "It might hurt the other ones' feelings."

That was so nice.

Secretly, Cody picked the fox.

Cody and Pearl brushed their teeth and got into their pj's. They snuggled into their sleeping bags. The pillow Pearl gave her was just right, not too fat and not too flat. It smelled like the same detergent Cody's mother used. Wait till she told Spencer how much fun sleepovers were!

"Sweet dreams!" Pearl's mother turned out the light.

Pearl's room went completely dark. It was like being inside a black jelly bean.

"You don't have a night-light?" said Cody.

"The smallest light keeps me awake."

"Oh." Cody unzipped her sleeping bag and started crawling around.

"What are you doing?" asked Pearl. "Are you okay?"

Cody found her backpack and reached inside. Crawl-crawl, she was back inside her sleeping bag.

"I just needed something," she said.

Snick! What do you know? Pearl had a pocket flashlight. Its beam shone straight in Cody's eyes.

"Oh, my goodness!" Pearl cried. "Is that the famous Gremlin?"

6
The Sleepover, Part 2

Pearl loved everything about Gremlin.

She loved his bumpy skin and pointy ears and terrible claws. She loved how he was made of indestructible material. She even liked the ant tattoo Cody had given him.

Pearl liking Gremlin was a surprise. Gremlin was the exact opposite of the soft, snow-white Arctic animals.

It just went to prove, Pearl was a person who thought for herself.

When they sneaked to the kitchen to get juice, Pearl brought Gremlin. When they thought up names for her band, she voted for the Gremlin Girls.

By now it had to be the middle of the night. Cody had never stayed up this late in her life. It was so much fun! It was so exciting! It was so possible she was getting a teeny bit tired! How could Pearl still be wide awake? On top of all her other talents, she possessed super-staying-awake powers.

"You hold the flashlight while I do an origami demonstration," Pearl whispered.

"Okay," Cody whispered.

Next thing she knew, Cody was waking up with her head on top of a pile of origami. Sunlight poured through the purple curtains. Pearl was asleep next to her, with Gremlin in her arms.

Cody's head felt funny. Like all her brains had leaked out and her head got filled with sand instead. Her eyes itched like they had mosquito bites.

If you are thinking this was not a great way to feel, *ding-ding!* You are right.

"Pearl," she whispered. "It's morning."

Pearl's eyes flew open. Then closed. Open. Closed. She groaned like a door in a haunted house.

"Pearl! Pearl!" Her baby brothers crawled in. One of them sucked on Cody's hair, and the other one drooled on her arm. Somebody's diaper smelled suspicious.

It crossed Cody's mind that a big brother might be better than a little one after all.

In fact, suddenly there was only one place in the whole wide world that she wanted to be. Home.

Pearl's mother made chocolate-chip pancakes. *No, thank you,* said Cody's stomach.

"I know two girls who didn't get enough sleep last night!" Pearl's mother smiled and waved her spatula. "Afternoon naps coming up!"

When Cody called to say she was ready to come home, her mother sounded strange. But maybe Cody's ears weren't working right, like all the rest of her body parts.

As Cody got dressed, her itchy eyes noticed something: Pearl was still holding Gremlin.

"I have an idea," said Pearl.

Something made Cody's sandbox brain go, *Uh-oh.*

"Let's trade toys."

Cody's beach brain did not understand.

"It's a twin thing to do!" Pearl explained. "Like

having sleepovers and telling secrets. You can pick any one of my Arctic animals you want."

"Wait. What?"

"I know you'll take good care of it. I can trust you." Pearl's forehead wrinkled. "I can, right?"

"I'm very trusty." Cody stood up straight.

"See? So which one do you want?"

Cody didn't even have to think.

"The fox," she said.

Pearl got it down from the shelf. She kissed its perky black nose.

"Foxy eats small mammals and berries. Her main predator is humans." Pearl whispered something in the fox's ear, then handed her over to Cody. "She is now in your care."

In this life, some things happen all by themselves while you just stand by with your mouth hanging open. Somehow, Cody held Arctic Fox and Pearl held Gremlin, and Pearl's mother was poking her head in the doorway, saying Cody's mother was here.

"Bye, Cody." Pearl made Gremlin wave a claw. "See you."

"Wait. I'm not sure if—"

"You promised!" Pearl's lip stuck out. "You said you were trusty!"

"I am! But—"

"Is everything all right?" Pearl's mother was back. "I think your mom's in a hurry, Cody."

"Okay."

Cody kissed Gremlin's bumpy green head, then staggered out the door.

7
Disaster

She hardly got her seat belt on before Mom hit the gas.

"Did you say thank you?" Mom asked.

"Yes." Well, she meant to.

"Did you have a good time?"

"Yes." Well, up till the last few minutes.

"Did you get any sleep?"

These were not good questions. Plus, Mom should be paying attention to the road. She nearly missed a stop sign. *Screech!* went the brakes.

"Mom! Have you got the whim-whams?"

"I'm sorry." Mom put her hand to her forehead. She wasn't wearing earrings. Not even lipstick! Something terrible was going on. "Wyatt went to visit Payton and—"

"You don't have to tell me. That brain pain broke his heart again."

"Don't call names."

"You drove past our house!"

"Oh, dear!" Mom backed up and made a sharp turn into the driveway. She shut off the car. "Please go talk to your brother, honey. Maybe you can help him."

Cody to the rescue! She ran upstairs. Wyatt's head was under his pillow.

"Hi, *amigo*! I'm home! Did you miss me?"

Headless Wyatt did not reply.

"I was at a sleepover, remember? Look what I got. An Arctic fox. It eats small mammals. Its main predator is humans."

Still no reply. Cody lifted a corner of the pillow. Arctic Fox nuzzled Wyatt's cheek.

"Waaa?" He grabbed the fox and stared at it with eyes of what-is-this-thing.

"I'm sorry P.U. smithereened your heart." Cody sat beside him on the bed. Wyatt swallowed so hard, she could hear it.

"It's not Payton's fault," he whispered.

"Yes it is! It's always her fault."

"I'm the one who forgot to lock it."

Wait. What?

Wyatt smooshed Arctic Fox to his chest. He did another noisy swallow.

"I rode over to say hi, and Payton asked me to come inside a minute. She made hot chocolate."

"With marshmallows?"

Wyatt nodded. He smooshed Arctic Fox so hard, she looked like a little fox rug.

"But when I came back out, the Cobra . . . was gone."

Cody was confused. "Where did it go?" she asked.

"What kind of dumb question is that?" hollered her brother. "It got stolen!"

"What? Are you sure?"

"Do bears poop in the woods?"

Cody went boneless. She slid onto the floor. How could someone do a thing like that? Didn't they know

how bad stealing was? Didn't they care that her big brother who never cried was making a gulping noise? A noise like someone who never cried but could not help it now?

Wyatt yanked the pillow back over his head.

"Just leave me alone, okay?" he said.

"No, *amigo*. Not okay."

Cody curled up at the bottom of his bed.

In this life, many things are catching:

Colds

Pink eye

Crying

She hugged Arctic Fox. Who was soft and squishy. And who got soggy when you cried on her.

Nothing like indestructible old Gremlin.

Thinking of him made Cody cry even harder.

8
Rule-Free

Dad called the cops.

It wasn't like on TV.

The policewoman who came looked regular. She reminded Cody of the woman who cleaned their teeth at the dentist. It was impossible to imagine her in a car chase, speeding around corners on two wheels.

She asked Wyatt a lot of questions. Including, "You say you left the bike unlocked?"

Wyatt's head hung down. "Yes," he said to his high-tops. "I forgot."

"Payton Underwood gets him all discombobulated," said Cody, but Mom shot her a look of that-is-so-not-helpful.

"I'll be honest with you." The policewoman stuck her notepad in her pocket and frowned. "We don't have much luck recovering stolen bikes."

"It's brand-new," Wyatt told his sneakers. "I paid for it myself."

"We'll do our best, kiddo."

The policewoman drove away. She didn't even turn on the siren.

"Search party," said Dad. "Saddle up."

Up and down and all around the neighborhood they drove. Dad asked everyone they saw to keep an eye out for a brand-new bike with COBRA on the side.

Cody got excited when she spotted a boy on a shiny black bike. But Wyatt took one look and shook his head.

Poor Wyatt. His heart was broken. Cody felt terrible.

Except. Except deep inside, in that place where she kept the things she wasn't supposed to feel, she was a tiny bit glad, too. Because now Wyatt couldn't zoom off and leave her in the dust anymore.

That night, Mom made Wyatt's favorite dinner — double cheeseburgers with unlimited chips. Wyatt stared at his plate like he forgot what food was for.

By now, Cody was so tired, she had to rest her head on the table. Nobody told her to mind her manners.

"If I ever catch the guys who did this, I'll punch their lights out," Wyatt said.

Their family was against violence. But nobody told Wyatt not to say that.

Mom put her arms around him.

A Non-Negotiable rule of Wyatt was no hugging. But Wyatt let her. For a long time.

It was a rule-free night.

This did not turn out to be as fun as you would think.

Rules can get on your last nerve. But at least you know what's supposed to happen. And what's not supposed to happen.

Cody never thought she'd agree with her rookie teacher, but having no rules felt strange. Even a little scary. Like, who is in charge here? And who knows what might happen next?

9
Cobra Quest

After school the next day, Spencer said he would help look for the bike. He wore the green-and-blue hat that GG had knitted him. It made his head look like a big, fuzzy globe.

"We should get Pearl, too," he said. "Three pairs of eyes are better than two."

Cody frowned. Pearl was not a person she felt like seeing right now, thank you very much.

"Pearl has eagle eyes," Spencer said.

"What's so great about eagles? Ants have compound eyes!"

"You said ants are better at smelling than seeing."

"Oh, fine," said Cody.

Pearl came right over. What was that in her arms? It looked like Gremlin. But Gremlin would never wear a fluffy pink scarf. And where Gremlin's tattoo should be, there was a purple Band-Aid.

"He had his tattoo removed," said Pearl.

"Gremlin doesn't need a scarf. He never gets cold."

"I'm not so sure about that." Pearl hugged Gremlin. "How's Foxy?"

Cody scrounged her brain. She tried to remember the last time she saw that squishy little thing.

"Remember to take her outside," said Pearl. "Cold is her natural habitat. Be careful not to get her fur dirty, though."

Spencer's fuzzy-globe head swiveled back and forth. He wore a look of I-can't-believe-it. He knew how deeply Cody and Gremlin loved each other. Oh, if only she'd listened to Spencer! If only she hadn't gone to that dumb sleepover, she'd still have Gremlin.

"We need a plan," Pearl said. "I think we should split up."

"I think we should stick together," Cody said.

"What do you think?" Pearl asked Spencer.

This was what is called a big mistake. Spencer took forever to make up his mind. You could grow a beard while you waited. If you were a man, that is.

At last, Spencer decided Pearl was right. They should split up, then meet back at GG's house.

"Fine." Cody pointed her finger at him. "But you better watch out. This neighborhood is crawling with dangerous bad guys!"

Spencer's eyes bugged. Cody felt bad. She didn't mean to scare him.

Well, maybe a little.

Cody marched down the sidewalk. The weather had turned colder overnight. The world was locked up in the deep freeze. One puffed-up bird sang its brave, lonesome song.

Cody marched on. She tried for eagle eyes. She tried for ant nose. But she didn't spy anything. And you can't really smell a bike.

By the time she got back to GG's, Cody was a human ice cube. Pearl and Spencer were already there. No luck either.

There was nothing to do but go inside and eat GG's fresh hot biscuits.

Pearl fed Gremlin some.

"Gremlin doesn't like biscuits," said Cody.

"Now he does," said Pearl.

Everything was wrong. Nothing was right. Pearl and Spencer were talking about music. They were going to play that ridiculous song "Green Sleeves" together in the winter concert. Cody sighed. She folded her hands on the table.

"What are you doing?" cried Pearl all of a sudden.

"Huh?"

Somehow, Cody's fingers had walked across the table. All by themselves, without permission. Somehow, they were slowly pulling Gremlin toward her. Pearl took him back.

"We made a deal," she said.

"I know," said Cody. "It's just that . . . Wyatt is sad. And he . . . he misses Gremlin."

"He does?" Pearl made a face of surprise. "I thought he said he was too old for toys!"

"Sometimes he makes mistakes."

"Do you want to go back on your solemn word?" Pearl asked.

In this life, some questions are impossible! Cody shook her head.

"I knew it." Pearl nodded. "I knew you were trusty!"

After Pearl went home, Cody, Spencer, and Mew-Mew sat on the porch swing. Usually, Cody liked to make the swing go fast, but today she didn't have the heart. Old-people slow, that's how they went. Swing . . . swing . . . swing . . .

Mr. Meen stomped outside in his bug-murderer boots. He took one look at them and roared, "Who died?"

Spencer explained about Wyatt's bike.

"Dang blast it!" Mr. Meen said. "That's a dirty rotten lawless shame! Thieves are worse than cockroaches!"

A rusty old car stopped at the curb. Molly and her little sister, Maxie, tumbled out. Maxie hugged their mother good-bye. Then she ran up onto the porch and hugged their father hello. She also hugged Cody, Spencer, and MewMew. Twice. How could such a sweet, cute hugging machine be related to Molly? In this life, there are many puzzles.

"Wyatt's bike got ripped off," said Mr. Meen. "I want you girls to keep an eye out for it."

Speaking of eyes, Molly's got a strange gleam.

Cody noticed. But she didn't think anything of it.

Not yet.

10
Stinking Cockroaches

For Journal Time, they had to write "What I Did Over the Weekend."

Gopal listed all the video games he played. Madison wrote the names of all the cousins she visited. Pearl's purple pencil was going a hundred miles an hour.

Probably she was writing how much she loved Gremlin. Cody grabbed her pencil. Without thinking, she wrote:

My weekend was so so bad. First somebody stole my best toy. Then somebody stole the cobra.

Cody gripped her pencil. She felt powerful. Also a little scared. Who knew writing could make you feel this way? Plus, once you got going, it was impossible to stop.

They are stinking rotten cockroaches!

"Cody," whispered Pearl. "Are you writing about our sleepover?"

Cody almost dropped her pencil. She covered her journal.

"Yes," she said.

"Me too!" Pearl smiled. "Can I read yours?"

At that moment, *gongggg*. Cody slapped her journal shut.

"Sorry," she said. "Journal Time is over!" She hurried to the front and put her journal in the basket.

Whew! Rules could certainly come in handy sometimes.

That night, Cody found Arctic Fox under Wyatt's bed, along with pizza crusts, stinky T-shirts, and a booklet called *Enjoy Your New Bike to the Max!*

Arctic Fox was covered with dust bunnies. Cody cleaned her up, but her perky face still looked sad.

"You miss Pearl, don't you? I bet you're homesick for your fellow Arctic creatures."

Cody made Foxy a bed of cotton balls, but it was no use. Her endangered heart was still heavy, Cody could tell.

Promises were promises. Everybody knew that. But what if a promise turned out to be a terrible mistake?

When Cody got her journal back the next day, there was no sticker. Instead there was:

Please see me at recess.

While the rest of the class went outside, Mr. Daniels tucked his shirt back in. He re-tied his shoes. He set a chair for Cody next to his desk.

His beautiful gong was only inches away. That thing was a finger magnet. Cody's fingers got such an itchy feeling, she had to sit on them.

"I'm so sorry about the robbery," Mr. Daniels said. "That's an awful thing to experience. You must be sad and angry."

Mr. Daniels understood! Of course he did. No

Stealing was an N-N rule if there ever was one. Cody felt a rush of friendly warmth for her teacher.

"I'm sure the police will do the best they can to help," he said.

"They don't have much luck finding Cobras," Cody told him.

He had a baby-smooth face, but now it crinkled up.

"Well," he said, "maybe your family can get something else instead. Something a little more . . . appropriate."

Just when they were starting to understand each other, he had to ruin things. Cody's hands flew out from underneath her. She waved them in the air.

"Wyatt loved the Cobra," she said. "My whole family did!"

"Yes, well, all families are different. I respect that." Mr. Daniels tried to smooth his hair, but it popped back up.

"At any rate," Mr. Daniels said, "I'm glad you

wrote about the robbery, Cody. I hope you continue to express your feelings. Writing helps us understand things. It can even make us feel better."

Cody wasn't so sure about that. But she could think of one thing that definitely would make her feel better. Gonging the gong. She stared at it with eyes of just-one-tap-please, but Mr. Daniels paid no attention. When it came to rules, he was as stubborn as a mule. A rule mule, that was Mr. Daniels.

11
Scene of the Crime

Cody and Wyatt made Cobra signs that said REWARD, NO QUESTIONS ASKED. They posted them all around Payton Underwood's neighborhood, the scene of the crime.

In normal times, Cody loved doing things with her big brother. But not today. *Trudge-trudge,* went Wyatt's feet. *Slump-slump,* went his shoulders. Whatever the total opposite of fun was, that was today.

"Ahoy!" called a too-familiar voice. "Avast, ye scurvy dogs!"

Molly and Maxie raced toward them. Maxie threw

her arms around Cody's knees. If Maxie were an animal, she'd be a koala.

"What are you doing in this neighborhood?" Molly demanded.

"This is where Wyatt's bike got stolen," said Cody. "What are *you* doing here?"

"This is where Mommy lives," said Maxie.

"Hey," said Wyatt. "If you see a bike with a race-face bash guard and WT-six-sixty-six wheels, let me know, okay?"

"I probably won't." Molly turned around and walked away.

"Won't see it or won't tell us?" Cody called.

If you are thinking Molly turned back and answered politely, you have not been paying attention.

Cody got a funny feeling. It was like that time she ate five pieces of pepperoni pizza and washed it down with a can of grape pop. Uneasy.

Only this time in her brain, not her stomach.

• • •

That night, Dad called from the road. He was a trucker. He was in Maine, picking up a shipment of wreaths and trees.

"The truck smells like Christmas," he told Cody. "Here, take a whiff."

What do you know? Cody could smell right through the phone! This was the miracle of Dad.

"How's your brother?" he asked.

"Not good. Not good at all."

"Poor cowboy."

"I hate whoever stole it!" Cody said, even though hating was not allowed in this family. "Why are people so evil?"

"Most people aren't, Little Seed. Look around. What do you see? People being good and kind and doing what they should."

"Not all the time."

"You're right. Now and then, everyone takes a wrong turn. They head down the wrong road."

"They should just turn around," said Cody.

"Most times they do. Most times they hang a U-ey and head back in the right direction."

Dad let her smell Christmas one more time, and then they said good night.

In bed, Cody tried to talk things over with Arctic Fox.

"Everybody around here misses something. Wyatt misses the Cobra. You miss Pearl, and I miss Gremlin. And my dad. It's like a lost and found, only no found."

Arctic Fox made no reply.

"What do you think Gremlin and Pearl are doing right now?"

Arctic Fox had no idea.

Arctic Fox was cute. But she had a lot of work to do in the conversation department.

12
Under Arrest!

At morning meeting, Mr. Daniels had a surprise.

Next week the class was going on a field trip!

Big deal.

Cody was not a field-trip fan. First they took you someplace exciting, with two zillion things to look at. Then they made you stay with your parent helper, absolutely no exploring or touching.

If you enjoy rules that make no sense at all, go on a field trip.

Then Mr. Daniels pronounced the words that changed everything.

"We'll be visiting the zoo's new Insectarium."

"Insects!" Pearl gave Cody a fist bump. "Your best thing!"

Mr. Daniels said their trip would fit right in with their new lesson — vertebrates and invertebrates.

Creatures with inside bones were called vertebrates. That included cats, horses, fish, and humans.

Creatures with no inside bones were called invertebrates. That included worms, amoebas, crabs, and *insects*.

When she got home, Cody went straight to her ant colony. She tapped the frozen ground to get their attention.

"Guess what? Invertebrates make up over ninety-eight percent of all life on Earth. You guys rule."

If only she could take the ants along on the field trip. Mr. Daniels said the Insectarium had bugs from every continent. The ants would enjoy seeing their relatives from across many lands.

He also told them the field-trip rules. These included: No Gum, Money, or Toys Allowed.

That probably meant no ants either.

Cody's toes were toe-sicles. She patted a leaf blanket over the ants. She hoped they were warm enough down there.

"I've been thinking," said Spencer the next day. "We should make a robber trap."

Cody halted in the middle of the sidewalk. Usually Spencer thought about things like his violin. Or how many minutes were in a year. Or if he could convince his parents to buy him more LEGOs. He was not what you'd call a dangerous, risky thinker.

Spencer explained how they'd put something valuable on the sidewalk, then hide and watch. When a robber tried to take it, they'd jump out and catch him.

"We can make a citizen's arrest," he said. "I saw it on TV."

And then he did a lot of blinking.

"It's a great plan," Cody said. "Only what do we have that's valuable?"

"I thought about that, too," he said. "First I thought GG's love beads. Then I thought my dad's golf clubs. But what if the robber gets away? So I decided it better be something that belongs to me."

By now they were at Spencer's house. Spencer went to his room and came back holding his violin case.

Cody's knees went weak. Spencer loved his violin up to the stars and down to the ocean floor. She couldn't believe he would risk it for her.

"My violin's not inside," he whispered.

Oh. But still! Only a true friend would do a thing like this. Cody touched her forehead to Spencer's and gave a little rub-a-dub-dub. That was how friendly ants greeted each other. It was ant for "Thank you for being my buddy in good times and bad."

They set the case on the sidewalk and hid on the porch to watch.

A boy rumbled past it on his skateboard.

A bird sat on it and *tra-la-la*ed.

Two teenage girls made the crazy sign with their fingers, then walked away giggling.

A man wearing a huge fur hat stopped. He removed the hat. He scratched his head.

Cody and Spencer traded looks. The man had a small mustache, exactly like a villain. Also, weren't his eyes kind of sneaky?

Under her breath, Cody practiced saying, "You are under arrest!"

The man looked around. And then he picked up
the case!

Cody leaped off the porch so fast the man jumped.
His hat fell off and landed by his foot, where it

huddled like a frightened, furry creature. But instead
of a quick getaway, he made a gentlemanly bow.

"Does this by any chance belong to you, my dear?"
he asked.

"It belongs to my best friend!"

"I'm glad there's no violin inside." He handed the case to her. "Cold is very bad for a sensitive instrument."

The man settled his hat back on his head. Then he lifted it back off and tipped it, like somebody in a black-and-white movie.

"Good day, my dear." He strolled away whistling.

"Mozart," said Spencer. "He's whistling Mozart." Spencer loved Mozart, who was a music-writer from ye olden days. "Bad guys don't whistle Mozart."

They carried the violin case back onto the porch. Cody heaved a sigh.

"I wish the trap worked," said Spencer. "When you're blue, I get blue, too."

"I know," she said. "I get blue when you're blue, too."

"I get blue when you're blue I'm blue."

"I get blue when you're blue I'm blue you're blue."

"I get—"

"Out of me way, land lubbers!" Molly blasted out her front door. She grabbed Spencer's scooter and shot off down the sidewalk.

Did she ask Spencer's permission?

Do bears use porta potties?

That six-slices-of-pepperoni feeling. Cody got it again.

13

The Insectarium

It was first thing in the morning, and Mr. Daniels's hair was already a wreck. Field Trip Day was upon them!

Madison had forgotten her bus-sickness medicine and was afraid she'd puke. She wrote MY PUKE BAG on a paper bag and clutched it tight. Gopal was on the floor being a Mutant Alien Scorpion. One of the parent helpers decided to have a baby instead of come on the trip.

On the bus, Cody and Pearl sat together. Pearl had a sneaky-peaky look.

"I have a secret," she whispered.

Pearl unzipped her backpack. She made her eyes go left-right, left-right. Wow. This must be a big secret, all right.

Now Pearl ducked down behind the seat in front of them. Cody ducked down, too.

When Pearl reached inside her backpack, Cody got a glimpse of something purple and sparkly.

"Are you ready?"

"Do bears — whoa!"

Cody could not believe her eyes. Gremlin! Pearl had brought him on the trip.

"What happened to him? He's all glittery."

"Shhh!" Pearl put her finger to her lips. "That's claw polish. Isn't it awesome?"

Gremlin looked so embarrassed. He was a fierce monster! He hated being glittery.

In a non-indoor voice, Cody said, "Don't you know the official field-trip rules?"

"Shhh!" Pearl almost slid off the bus seat. She

zipped Gremlin back inside, then sat up straight. Left-right, left-right went her rule-following eyes.

"I don't know what came over me." Pearl bit her lip. "I just couldn't help it."

"You took a wrong turn."

"Right."

"No, wrong."

Pearl folded her hands in her lap. She looked worried.

"I won't take him out," she whispered. "I won't even look at him again, I promise."

Cody's heart did a little dip. Pearl looked so sorry. She was a rule-follower, not a rule-breaker. She didn't mean to do wrong.

But she really, really, *really* should not have stuck glitter on Gremlin's claws.

The Insectarium was swarming.

With kids.

With bugs.

With excitement.

Mr. Daniels showed them the display of leaf-cutter ants. All the ants had jobs, he explained. Some gathered leaves. Some chewed up the leaves, then fed the pulp to their fungus gardens. Some were garbage collectors. And some were in the army.

"That would be me!" said Gopal.

The class watched the ants march back and forth through their tunnels. To keep the walls from caving in, Mr. Daniels said, the ants smoothed them with their own saliva. This was the nice word for spit.

Madison was not enjoying this.

"Can't we see something cute instead? Like pandas?" She looked around. "And what is that hissing noise? There better not be any snakes in here!"

"No snakes." Mr. Daniels smiled, like for once he was enjoying himself. Could he be a fellow bug-lover? "Follow me." He led them toward a large glass tank. The closer they got, the louder the hissing grew.

Madison took one look and almost fainted.

"Dude!" cried Gopal. "Those guys are massive!"

"Behold," said Mr. Daniels. "The Madagascar hissing cockroach."

Reddish-brown bugs the size of baby carrots scurried around the tank. Some peeked from under leaves. Some climbed up the glass. A few were fighting, or something. Those were the ones making all the noise.

"Most invertebrates make noise by rubbing body parts together," said Mr. Daniels. "But these fellows blow through air holes, just like us vertebrates. Their native habitat is an island off the coast of Africa."

One of the cockroaches crawled up the glass and looked right at Cody. It had horns and fat, hairy legs. Its long antennas waved gracefully.

Hiss. Hiss.

"Why does everyone say cockroaches are gross?" asked Cody.

"Because," said Pearl. "Most people don't think for themselves."

Cody made a mental note to ask Mr. Meen not to insult cockroaches any more.

There were so many wondrous bugs, it was impossible to pick her favorite. The giant walking stick, which looked exactly like its name? The luna moth, which looked like it was wearing an evening gown?

"Why choose?" said Pearl. "Just love them all equally."

That was a lot of bug love. Cody smiled.

They ate lunch, and watched a movie called *Bug Out!* Too soon it was time to go home.

Quick-quick, Cody ran for a last look at the hissing cockroaches. One still stuck to the glass. Maybe he was trying to escape. That gave Cody's heart a pinch. Maybe he longed for his island home, thousands of miles away.

"There you are!" A parent helper came rushing up. "Cody, you know the rule is to stay with your group at all times!"

"I'm sorry."

As she turned away, the cockroach waved his long antennas. Cody waved sadly back.

The class was putting on coats and getting backpacks. Where was Pearl?

"I can't wait to get out of here," said Madison. "I feel like bugs are crawling all over me."

Cody's backpack hung beside Pearl's. Who was still nowhere in sight.

Cody was a trusty person who would never go back on her word.

But she felt sad about that cockroach. She needed Gremlin to cheer her up. Quick-quick, she unzipped Pearl's backpack. One tender pat, that was all!

Well, maybe just one little hug.

To her surprise, Gremlin waved his claws. This was monster for "Help! Help me return to my real home!"

What could Cody do? Nothing, that's what. Gremlin belonged to Pearl now. Cody had to put him back, and she did. Only, oops, somehow she put him inside *her* backpack. Big mistake. And now she saw Pearl coming out of the restroom. *Zip-zip!* Cody closed both backpacks.

"You know what I was thinking?" said Pearl. "What if bugs look at humans and think, 'Ooh, weird. Ooh, creepy'?"

"Ha-ha! That is so funny!" Cody's voice squeaked like it needed oil.

"Are you okay?" Pearl looked at her.

Cody could only nod. Her voice was out of service.

On the bus home, the boys did Madagascar

cockroach hisses. It got so loud, Mr. Daniels put them on Zone Zero. Not a peep!

That made it really easy to hear Madison puke into her bag.

Cody looked out the window. She hugged her backpack tight. That ride took two zillion years.

14
Hand Attack

At home, Cody scrubbed off the purple glitter. She gave Gremlin a new tattoo of a luna moth. Gremlin waved his sparkle-free claws. This was monster for, "Thank you for rescuing me. You are my hero."

That night when she and Gremlin got under the covers, Cody's foot touched something squishy. Arctic Fox. Cody pulled her out and introduced her to Gremlin.

Now she had both toys.

That wasn't fair, was it?

But Gremlin belonged with her, didn't he?

Except Pearl was going to be so upset, wasn't she?

It was like Cody was having an argument, only how could that be? Nobody else was here.

Outside the cold wind blew. A branch *tap-tapped* against her window. And just then, a memory *tap-tapped* inside her.

Now and then, everyone takes a wrong turn, she heard Dad say. *But you can always hang a U-ey and head back in the right direction.*

The next morning, Pearl was late for school. When she finally arrived, her sweater was buttoned wrong. And she had forgotten her homework.

These were unnatural events.

"Something happened," she whispered to Cody.

Cody felt a heavy, invisible hand on her shoulder.

"What?" she whispered back.

"I'll tell you at recess."

The day was super windy. Leaves twirled. Hats

flew. Scarves streamed out like flags. Pearl clasped her mittens under her chin.

"I don't know how to tell you this, but . . . Gremlin got stolen."

"What?" Spencer pulled off his fuzzy-globe hat. He shook his head like he couldn't hear right. "Another robbery?"

"I promised not to take him out of my backpack and I didn't. I waited till I got home." Pearl's face folded up like origami. "And he was gone!"

The wind was trying to knock them over. It hissed like a herd of cockroaches.

"Who knows who took him? There were so many kids. My mother says we probably won't get him back." Pearl's voice quivered. Tears rolled down her cheeks. "I'm sorry, Cody! I never should have taken him on the trip."

"It's not your fault," said Spencer. "Whoever took him is the bad guy. Right, Cody?"

"Umm . . ."

Pearl wiped her eyes, but the tears kept spilling over. Cody reached into her pocket.

"Guess what?" she said.

Pearl did a gasp. She pressed her mittens to her heart.

"Foxy!" she cried.

Cody had done her best to get the dust bunnies

off. Also the spot of grape jelly. And the ketchup. She had brushed the fur with one of Mom's special makeup brushes.

"You can have her back," said Cody. "I even brought the cotton-ball bed I made her. See?"

Pearl kissed Arctic Fox on the nose. She stroked the fluffy tail and perky ears.

"You took good care of her," said Pearl. "I knew you were a trusty person."

"Anyway!" said Cody. "I brought her since you don't have Gremlin anymore."

Pearl was smiling. Her eyes were shining. She was a fountain of happiness!

But wait. Something was wrong. Her smile began to fade.

"How did you know I didn't have Gremlin anymore?" she asked.

"Huh? What?" Cody had never been struck by lightning, but she was pretty sure this was how it felt.

Pearl looked at her for a long moment. Then she bit her lip.

"Never mind," she said. "For a second there I thought . . . But you'd never. You're not like that."

"Like what?" Spencer looked so confused.

It was hard to speak when you were electrified.

"Thank you, Cody," Pearl said. "I know you're trying to be nice, but it wouldn't be fair to take Foxy back. My conscience would never let me rest."

Pearl ran to line up. Even though it wasn't time yet.

"What's a conscience?" Cody asked Spencer.

"I'm not sure." He tugged his hat back on. "Something that keeps you awake. Maybe a really loud noise? Or a bad stomachache?"

Speaking of stomachaches. Molly came running up, with little Maxie close behind.

"Ooh!" cried Maxie when she saw Arctic Fox. She petted the soft white fur. "It's so adorbs!"

"My sister needs to borrow that." Molly tried to grab it, but Cody was faster than she was. She and Spencer took off, the mean wind whipping their faces.

At Journal Time, they had to write about the Insectarium.

Cody picked up her pencil. She smoothed the new page. She wrote:

The Insectarium.

Her hand started hurting. It was having a hand attack. She had to put her pencil down.

"I don't feel like writing about it, either," whispered Pearl. "But we have to."

Pearl's rule-following hand got to work.

Cody picked her pencil back up. She put it back down. She peeked at Pearl's journal. Pearl's usual handwriting was perfect. She never erased. But today, her paper had an ugly smudge in the middle.

Cody picked up her pencil again. *Write about the leaf-cutter ants,* she commanded her hand.

But her hand would not listen. It refused to do automatic pilot writing. Instead, it wrote:

I hated it. Bugs should not be in cages. It is no way to live.

Gongggg!

As Cody put her journal in the basket, Mr. Daniels gave her a smile of we-have-so-much-in-common.

"Wasn't the Insectarium great?" he said. "I can't wait to read what you wrote about it."

Sometimes your head gets so heavy, your neck bone can't do its job. You might as well be a spineless invertebrate.

15
Snow Globe

In this life, some questions are easy:

How much is 2 + 2?

Can you spell "cat"?

Do you want to go to your room right this minute?

And some are hard:

Which are cuter, dolphins or pandas?

Which are cooler, zombies or vampires?

What Wyatt asked Cody that night.

December was a busy month for Mom. Everyone wanted new boots and new party shoes and new slippers to give for presents, so the shoe department was a nuthouse. As Head of Shoes, Mom often had to work late. When Dad was on the road, that meant Wyatt was in charge.

Tonight, he was supposed to heat up the leftover casserole for their dinner.

In case you forgot, here is a reminder: cooking was not on Mom's list of talents.

Dad was the only living human who could eat her cabbage-and-hot-dog casserole. And even he turned greenish.

Wyatt took the casserole out of the refrigerator. He looked at it with eyes of tragedy.

"We could make mac and cheese instead," said Cody. "I bet Mom wouldn't mind."

So Wyatt stirred some up. He set it on the table and handed her a fork.

"No eating out of the pot," she said. "No earbuds at the table."

"Rule-free night," he said.

No toys at the table—that was another rule. Cody ran to get Gremlin. He sat on her lap while they ate.

"Why does food taste more delicious from the pot than on a plate?" Cody asked her brother.

In reply he gave a burp.

"And why do you have to say 'excuse me' when you burp, like you did something wrong? But when you sneeze people bless you?"

"Rules don't always make sense," said Wyatt.

"That's what I think!" Cody hugged Gremlin. "Wyatt, do you ever wish you didn't give me Gremlin?"

"At first." Wyatt forked up a giant macaroni clump. "I used to sneak into your room and play with him."

"You did?"

"Don't tell anybody!" Wyatt waggled the clump at her. "That's classified info."

"But I'd do the same thing. I mean, if by some horrible mistake I ever gave Gremlin away . . . Aack!" A piece of macaroni got stuck in her throat. She took a big swallow of milk. "I'd want him back, too. I might . . . who knows? I might even steal him back."

Wyatt was busy scraping out the bottom of the pot.

"But it wouldn't be stealing, would it?" Cody asked. "If he belonged to me?"

"I don't know, *amiga*," Wyatt said. "How would you like it if I took Gremlin back?"

There it was! *How-would-you-like-it-if* questions were the hardest of all.

"Hmm." Cody looked around. "I wonder if there's any dessert."

"I keep thinking about who swiped my bike." Wyatt took his earbuds out. This was a signal he was really, truly talking to you. "Maybe someone poor who never got to have a bike. Or maybe somebody whose own bike got stolen."

"That still doesn't make it right," said Cody.

"I know. But I like to understand things. I like to know the reasons for things." Wyatt rested his chin on the palm of his hand. "I wonder if his conscience ever bothers him."

"What is a conscience, anyway?"

"You know. That feeling that tells you if you did the wrong or the right thing."

Oh. *That* feeling.

"Like, at first, you might be all excited because you stole this insanely cool bike and got away with it," Wyatt went on. "But after a while, your conscience starts to surface. You start thinking, what did I do?"

Some feelings were simple: Happy. Scared. Those feelings were right on top, right out in the open.

But conscience must be deep down. Like a backbone. Conscience must be a vertebrate.

"Thank you for not stealing Gremlin," she said.

"Better keep an eye on him." Wyatt grinned. "I still might."

"What?"

"Just kidding!"

Wyatt put his earbuds back in. Thus ended their conversation.

After that, Cody kept a careful eye on Gremlin.

Because even though Wyatt was a trusty person, what if he wasn't?

These days, it was hard to be sure.

Later, Dad called from the road.

Cody was full of questions for her father. They whirled around inside like she was a shook-up, human snow globe. Questions like: What if you tried to do a U-turn but it didn't work? And is it still stealing if it's your own stuff? And how old do you have to get before life stops being so complicated?

But it had been a long day. Again. And all those questions seemed too hard. So instead she said, "I wish we knew who took the Cobra."

"Me too, Little Seed."

In this life, not all wishes come true. But sometimes, even if you didn't crack the wishbone, or blow out all the candles in one breath, or spot the first star — sometimes it happens.

Here is the proof. The next day, Cody knew who the bike robber was.

16
A Wish Come True

Pearl was still a friend to all, and especially to Cody.

But something had changed.

Pearl had lost her oomph.

They were working on their vertebrate/invertebrate projects. Madison was printing out information. Only the article turned out to be 163 pages long. Mr. Daniels kept hitting CANCEL, but it would not stop printing. His hair waved wildly.

"He should use more product on that cowlick," Pearl whispered to Cody.

"Cowlick?" Cody cracked up. "It's called a cow-lick? That's so disgusting."

"I know!" cried Pearl. And she cracked up, too.

For one whole minute, it was just like old times.

Then Pearl went oomph-less again.

Mr. Daniels didn't believe in already-friends being partners. He believed in future-friends working together.

So Cody was stuck with Gopal, who had no respect for bugs. Unless they were toxic beetles. Or former humans with super spider powers. When Cody explained how strong and loyal ants were, he did a laugh of scorn.

"Ants?" he said. "I could smoosh a hundred ants easy!"

Pearl would never say such a thoughtless thing. Cody missed Pearl, even though she was right there. How could this be? It was a mystery. Not a good one.

You might think Mr. Daniels would get distracted by 163 pages of vertebrate facts. You might think he would forget all about Journal Time, but think again. *Gongggg!* When Cody got her journal, she slid off her chair to sit under the table. What had Mr. Daniels written this time? Opening it up, she read:

> The zoo keeps its animals in safe, appropriate environments, just the way you kept your cobra in a tank.

Cody peeked out from under the table to make sure her teacher hadn't gotten replaced by a nuthouse person. Nope. There he was at his desk, guarding his N-N gong same as always.

"Cody," he said. "Bottoms on Chairs, Minds on Work!"

With a sigh, she climbed back into her chair.

"Mr. Daniels thinks we kept the Cobra in a tank," she whispered to Pearl.

"Teachers inhabit a different world," Pearl whispered back. She set down her pencil. "Speaking of the Cobra?"

Cody shook her head.

"Poor Wyatt." Pearl hunched her shoulders up to her ears. "Now I know what it's like to be an innocent victim of crime."

Cody decided this was an excellent time to sharpen her pencil. The sharpener was by the door. As she used it, Molly's class went by. Molly was busy poking the wimpy boy in front of her, but now she pointed at Cody.

"Thar she blows!"

Cody made her names-will-never-hurt-me face. Why was Molly like that? Her conscience must be buried really deep inside. It must be in the vicinity of her intestines, which was the scientific word Wyatt had taught her for guts.

If Molly even had a conscience at all.

Inside Cody's mind, pictures of poor Wyatt and evil Molly whirled around. They got dizzy and bumped together. And just like that, *kapow!* It was an explosion in there.

Gongggg!

Cody speed-walked to her desk. Grabbing her journal, she scribbled:

The cobra could not fit in a tank. It was way too big.

She tossed the journal in the basket. The minute school was over, she ran to find Spencer.

"Come on," she said, grabbing his hand. "We are going to make a citizen's arrest."

17
Citizen's Arrest

Cody couldn't believe it had taken her so long to put all the clues together.

She and Spencer were watching Molly zoom up and down the sidewalk on his scooter. Maxie sat on the porch swing, singing "99 Bottles of Beer on the Wall." This was not what you'd call an interesting song, especially since Maxie could hardly count forward, let alone backward. But MewMew seemed to like it. Possibly because she was deaf.

"Take one down and pass it around!" sang Maxie.

"Are you sure about this?" *Blink-blink* went Spencer's eyes.

"It has to be her," said Cody. "She's always taking stuff that isn't hers. And her mother lives near the scene of the crime."

"*Seventy-eleven bottles of beer on the wall!*" sang Maxie.

"We don't have any evidence," said Spencer. "You need evidence to make an arrest. I'm pretty sure that's a rule."

Not another rule! But it was too late now. Molly was barreling toward them.

"Out of me way, bilge rats!"

Cody held up her hand. "You are hereby under arrest!" she said.

Molly stopped the scooter. She looked confused.

"What did you say?"

"We are making a citizen's arrest for stealing." Cody went up on her toes. "And you better give my brother's bike back!"

Shocked, that was how Molly looked now. So shocked and surprised that something inside Cody wobbled, like a tall vase on the edge of a table. In an earthquake.

"I didn't take his bike," Molly said. "I'd never do a thing like that!"

Maxie stopped singing. She ran to stand beside her big sister.

"You better back off right now," said Molly.

"Back off!" echoed Maxie.

They folded their arms. They glared.

The vase inside Cody wobbled again. But she folded her own arms back.

"Well then, prove you didn't take it."

"If I took it, where is it?" said Molly. "Do you see a bike anywhere?"

"No!" said Maxie. "I do not!"

"Maybe . . ." Cody said. "Maybe it's at your mother's house."

"Fine! Follow me."

Molly boosted Maxie into a piggyback and sped off down the street.

Spencer ran to get permission from GG, then he

and Cody tried to catch up. Even with Maxie on her back, Molly's middle name was *Fast*. By the time they got to the house, everyone was out of oxygen.

The garage had the kind of door you have to open yourself. It hung so crooked, Molly and Maxie had to bend their knees and shove with all their might to raise it.

The garage was as junky as Cody's. Only worse. Broken chairs, old windows, smooshed pool toys — junk everywhere. In the corner leaned an ancient bike with no seat and two flat tires.

It was not the Cobra.

If the Cobra had an opposite, it was that bike.

The tall, precious vase inside Cody teetered on the very edge.

"See?" said Molly. "I told you!"

"We told you!" said Maxie.

Molly pressed her lips into a thin line. Her eyes grew strangely shiny. Suddenly, she turned her back on them.

"I'm not really a pirate, you know." Her voice was so small, you could hardly hear her. "I would never, ever steal."

"Don't cry!" Maxie fastened herself to her big sister. "Molly, don't cry."

Crash! The vase inside Cody fell off the table.

"I'm sorry!" she said. "I'm really sorry. I take it back. I made a mistake."

Molly would not turn around. Her shoulders went up and down. Cody felt terrible. Worse than terrible. The broken vase was poking her insides. Ow, ow.

"How would you like it if someone called you a robber?" asked Molly.

"I wouldn't! I wouldn't like it at all."

"Me either," said Maxie. Now she gave Cody a tender pat. "It's all right. Don't be sad, Cody."

But Cody was. They all were. It was a march of sadness the whole way back to GG's house. As soon as they got there, Molly picked up Spencer's scooter and zoomed away. Maxie sat on the steps and sucked her thumb.

"I just thought," Cody told Spencer, "the way she's always taking your stuff without asking, I just thought—"

"She gives it back sooner or later," said Spencer. "And I can share. I mean, I have lots more stuff than they do."

The truth of this gave Cody's heart a painful twang. Molly and Maxie didn't have much good stuff. And Molly would really love a bike like the Cobra.

But she did not steal it. She never would.

Cody was very sorry she'd made a mistake.

But she was glad, too.

Toss-turn, toss-turn. That night, Cody couldn't sleep. The cold wind blew and that branch tapped against her window. It was trying to remind her of something.

Cody pulled the covers over her head. But just then, she heard the voice of Mr. Daniels. *Writing can help us understand things.*

Could her rookie rule-mule teacher be right?

Cody found some paper and a pencil. Writing in the dark was exciting, like being a member of a secret society. At last, her eyes got heavy. She tucked the paper into the pillow cave and fell asleep.

In the morning, she tried to read her in-the-dark writing. Lines and squiggles covered the paper.

It looked like a hissing cockroach had written it with his antenna.

Sometimes writing can help you figure things out. But other times, you can't figure out your own writing.

And yet, something had happened in the night. Something had changed. Cody pulled Gremlin from his cave of pillows.

"I have to ask you a question," she said.

Gremlin gazed back with eyes of patience.

"It's a hard one," Cody warned him.

Gremlin gazed back with eyes of trust.

"I don't want to be a robber anymore. Would it be okay if . . . what would you think if . . . if I gave you back to Pearl?"

Gremlin slowly waved his claws. This was monster for, "It is the right thing to do."

"Except, when Pearl finds out I'm a robber, she won't want to be friends anymore. Then I won't have you. And I won't have her, either."

For once, Gremlin was out of answers.

As usual, Arctic Fox had nothing to say.

That left it up to Cody. She tried again to read her nighttime writing, hoping for a clue. It still looked like hieroglyphics, which is writing from the time of mummies.

But wait. Maybe writing was the answer after all.

Quick-quick, Cody got dressed. Using her right hand to disguise her handwriting, she wrote a note. She wanted to run straight to Pearl's house, but she wasn't allowed to go that far alone. Cody's rule-breaking days were over. From now on, she was going to do everything right.

She and Gremlin hurried down the hall to wake up Wyatt.

18
The Plan

"Wait till Mom gets home," Wyatt grumbled. "She'll take you."

"That will be too late."

Wyatt did major groaning. "What is this, life or death?"

Not exactly. But Cody had the feeling that if she didn't do her plan right now, this minute, she might change her mind. And she did not want that to happen.

"Please!" she said. "I'll give you my bendy-straw collection."

"Oh, wow. An offer I can't refuse."

Wyatt dragged himself out of bed. He washed his face with his anti-pimple soap, and did his chin-ups, and ate approximately three boxes of cereal. If you think a snail, which is an invertebrate, is slow, that is because you never saw Wyatt in the morning. But did Cody complain?

Well, maybe a little.

Cody put Gremlin and her note inside a bag. She and Wyatt wheeled their bikes out of the garage. Wyatt looked at his old bike with eyes of gloom.

"Remind me why we're doing this," he said.

"I have to drop off something. It will only take a second."

As they rode, Cody looked up and saw a nest tucked high in the crook of a tree. You wouldn't be able to spy it in summer, when the branches were covered in leaves. It felt as if the tree was sharing a secret. Cody smiled.

Riding bikes with her big brother was so

wonderful. Even though the day was cold, Cody's heart felt like it was wrapped up in a warm, un-itchy scarf. Wyatt loved to sleep, but he had gotten up. He didn't like his old bike, but he was riding it. Just for her.

Cody's eyes got a little watery. Good old Wyatt! She wished the two of them could just ride on and on, side by side, forever and ever.

Except here was Pearl's house.

In this life, making a plan is easy.

Doing it, not so much.

Nobody was outside. Cody knew Pearl had piano lessons on Saturday mornings, so the coast would be clear. All she had to do was jump off her bike, run up to the front door, set down the bag, run back to her bike, jump on, and ride away.

"What's in that bag, anyway?" Wyatt asked.

"Oh, nothing."

"We came all this way for nothing?"

"I'll be right back."

Cody tiptoed up the front walk. All was quiet. Nothing stirred. She hugged the bag with Gremlin inside. She longed to take him out for one last farewell and, oops, she did.

Just as the front door flew open. There stood Pearl. Her baby brothers peeked around her legs. When they saw Cody they broke into baby cheers.

"Cody!" Pearl had a look of surprise. "What are . . ."

That was when she noticed Gremlin.

Times a hundred. That's how much Pearl's surprise got multiplied. At least.

Cody's own surprise was pretty much off the surprise chart.

"You're home?" she said.

"Gremlin!" Pearl said. "I can't believe it! You got him back! Justice is served! Hooray!"

"Hooway!" The babies clapped. One of them started sucking on Cody's pant leg.

"Where was he, Cody?"

"Umm," said Cody. "Umm, don't you have piano?"

"My teacher is sick so my lesson is canceled." Pearl opened the door wider. "Come on in."

"Umm . . . my brother's waiting for me." Cody pointed at Wyatt.

Who was standing perfectly still, like one of those

pointer dogs. His hand shaded his eyes, and he was squinting down the street.

"Who did it?" Pearl asked. "Who stole Gremlin?"

At that exact moment, Wyatt let out a blood-curdling yell. Cody spun around. Her brother's arms were a windmill.

Somebody was riding by. On a shiny black bike that looked very familiar.

"Stop!" Wyatt yelled. "Give me back my bike, you amoeba!"

The rider sped up.

"Cody!" Wyatt cried. "Stay here with Pearl. Don't move till I come back!"

With that, he took off.

"Is that the Cobra?" cried Pearl.

"Cobwa!" squeaked the twins.

Cody watched her brother stand up on the pedals of his old bike. Its wheels spun, and so did her heart. How could Wyatt ever catch up to the Cobra with its WT666 wheels and race-face bash guard?

And what if he did? What would that conscience-less robber do to him?

"Come inside," said Pearl. "We better tell my mother."

In this life, sometimes you know what you're supposed to do, and you do it.

Other times, you know what you're supposed to do, but that doesn't make any difference.

Cody handed Gremlin to Pearl.

"I have to help Wyatt," she said.

As Cody rode away, the babies cheered. Or maybe they cried. Cody couldn't tell.

19
The Chase

Wyatt's old bike was going as fast as it could, which turned out to be pretty fast. Cody could hardly keep him in sight.

Up the street. Around the corner. Cody's legs pump-pump-pumped.

The Cobra hung a right with Wyatt close behind.

Pump-pump-pump. *How long do you expect us to keep this up?* her legs demanded. But Cody didn't slow down. She couldn't. Instead, she stiffened her vertebrate backbone.

Wyatt had left her in the dust. But he needed her. She knew he did.

At the next corner, the Cobra and Wyatt shot straight ahead. Cody had to wait till a car went by. Then another one. Then another. It was practically a parade of cars! She was stuck waiting till it was safe to cross.

Looking around, she realized she was near Payton Underwood's house.

In fact, there Payton was now. Her shampoo-commercial hair streamed behind her.

"Cody? What's happening? Was that Wyatt's bike?"

Cody's breath was still trying to catch up with the rest of her. Before she could answer, pounding footsteps made her turn around again.

"Shiver me timbers!" yelled Molly. "Is that the bike brigand? I'll run him through!"

"Me too!" yelled Maxie.

At last, no cars. Looking both ways, they all

charged across the street. By now,
Wyatt was down the end of the block.
It was hard to see exactly what was happening.

"Wyatt!" Cody yelled. "Here I come!"

She ducked her head. She pumped her legs. When
she looked up again, someone was running away.

And the someone was not Wyatt.

"You did it!" Cody leaped off her bike. She plopped
onto her bungie. Her legs had turned to Jell-O.

"What the?" Her brother helped her up. "I told
you to stay put." He dusted her off. "Are you okay?"

"The Cobra!" said Cody. "You got it back."

Molly and Maxie were right behind her. Next came Payton, her cheeks glowing rosebud pink.

"OMG? OMG?" She gasped. "That was so thrilling? Like a car chase in the movies, only with bikes?"

But something strange was going on. Wyatt just stood there. Why didn't he look happy?

"Are you okay?" Cody asked. "The robber didn't hurt you, did he?"

"No. He lost control and crashed into that fire hydrant. Then he ran."

"Poor bikey," said Maxie.

That was when Cody noticed. The Cobra's front tire was flat. And the seat was crooked.

"We can fix it," she said. "I'll help you."

"It's not that," her brother said. He rubbed the side of his face. "All of a sudden, I'm not sure if it's really my bike. There's more than one Cobra in the world. What if that kid thought I was trying to steal his bike? And he got so scared he crashed and ran away? And now *I'm* a robber."

They all looked at one another.

"Oh," said Payton. "That would be terrible?"

But Cody knew how to tell for sure whose bike it

was. Kneeling down, she examined the snaky letters on the side. Sure enough.

"Look." She pointed to the O. "See how the paint is chipped so it looks like a heart? See how it says *C-heart-BRA?*"

Silence fell. For two seconds.

"Bra!" yelled Molly. "Did you say *bra?*"

Payton's cheeks turned the color of cherry cough medicine.

"What in the world are you talking about?" cried Wyatt.

Always Tell the Truth. This is a top ten rule. Probably the best thing is to tell it right away, on the spot.

But here is something important to know. The truth is not like those foods you have to throw away after they get too old. The truth does not have an expiration date.

Cody told Wyatt about crashing his bike in the driveway and chipping the paint. When she finished, he stared at her for a moment. A very long moment. And then he raised his hand.

He was going to put her in a Houdini headlock. Or worse.

"You are unbelievable," he said.

And then he gave her a high five.

In this life, many things are catching:

Colds

Crying

High fives

Next thing you knew, it was a high-five festival. Even Molly high-fived Cody.

Too hard. But still.

Wyatt had to walk the Cobra back. Cody had to ride her bike back. That left his old bike.

"I'll take it to my mother's." Without asking permission, Molly set Maxie on the seat and rode away. Fast.

20
The Other Robber

When Cody and Wyatt got home, the phone was ringing. Wyatt answered.

"It's Pearl."

Pearl! Cody had forgotten all about her.

"Did you catch him?" Pearl asked. "Did you catch the crook?"

In the background, the twins chirped, "Cwook! Cwook!"

Cody told her everything.

"I can't believe it," Pearl said. "You got the Cobra back, and you rescued Gremlin."

Cody's legs were getting that Jell-O feeling again. She had to sit down.

"Stop it, you two," said Pearl. "Don't eat the robber's note!" Now she read it in the deep, scary voice of a robber. "*'You can have him back. Do not ask any questions. From, The Robber.'*"

The Jell-O feeling got hold of Cody's stomach.

"He must have been so mean," said Pearl. "Or she. I guess it could have been a girl robber. Plus, he or she has terrible handwriting. Cody, aren't you going to tell me what happened?"

Wobble-wobble. One enormous bowl of Jell-O, that was Cody.

"Cody? Are you there?"

Only two creatures knew who the Robber was. Her and Gremlin. And Gremlin would never tell.

"Are you still upset?" Pearl asked. "You don't have to be, not anymore. Everything's okay now."

Pearl was so nice! She might be the nicest, trustiest person in the whole world. Tears spurted out of Cody's eyes. She couldn't lie to Pearl a single second longer. If only Always Tell the Truth would work for the second time that day.

"Pearl," she whispered. "I'm the Robber."

"Hee, hee! Good joke."

"Hee, hee." The babies giggled in the background.

"For real," whispered Cody. "I'm the one who stole Gremlin."

Pearl drew a breath. A breath as deep as the ocean.

"Are you telling me that *you* took him out of my backpack?"

All Cody could do was nod.

"You had him all this time? And you didn't tell me?"

Cody nodded. Then she shook her head. Who knew what the right answer was?

Pearl was quiet for such a long time, Cody wondered if the phone had gotten broken.

She sort of hoped it had.

But no, Pearl was still there. And now she did something extremely un-Pearl.

Pearl the rule follower. Pearl the friend to all. Pearl the perfect and polite, the trusty and the true.

She hung up. *Click.*

Without even saying good-bye.

That night, Cody dreamed she was driving a eighteen wheeler just like Dad's. It was fun cruising down the highway, singing along with the radio.

Until she made a wrong turn. She found herself on a dark, twisty road full of holes. *Bump-bump*—the truck. *Thump-thump*—her heart.

"Little Seed?"

Cody's eyes popped open. Dad was sitting on

her bed! He wasn't due till morning. Cody pinched herself to make sure it wasn't a dream. Ouch!

"I made good time getting home," he said softly. "Were you having a bad dream?"

Cody's heart was still thumpy. She burrowed deep into the cave of Dad.

"Want to tell me?" he asked.

Outside, the cold wind blew. In Dad's arms, Cody felt like she was in a house inside a house, safe as safe could be. At first, she had trouble getting the words out, but then they started coming faster and faster, till they stuck together like bubbles from a bubble blaster. She told Dad about trading Gremlin and Arctic Fox. About stealing Gremlin back, and trying to un-steal him. About Pearl hanging up without saying good-bye.

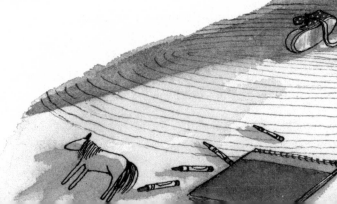

Dad gave a low whistle.

"Let me get this straight," he said. "Pearl has Gremlin now."

"Uh-huh."

"You told her what you did. And that you were sorry."

"Uh-huh."

"You made a mistake. Maybe two. Or three. And then you did everything you knew to set them right."

"But I didn't. It's still a big horrible mess and Pearl will never be my friend again."

"Don't let anybody tell you that doing the right thing is easy. Lots of times, it's flat-out hard."

Cody leaned against her father's chest. She could feel his heart beating.

"That's why I'm so proud of you for trying, Little Seed."

"But Dad? Something else."

"What's that?"

"When the Cobra got stolen, I was a little bit happy."

"You were?"

"Uh-huh. Because I don't want Wyatt to leave me in the dust."

"Ahh." Dad got quiet. Then he cleared his throat. "Can I tell you a secret?"

"Okay."

"When I see how fast you and Wy are growing, I think, wow. Look at them speeding down the highway of life. And I feel proud and happy. But sometimes I wish I could tap the brakes. Sort of slow things down a bit. I wish I could keep you both little a while longer."

Cody pressed her cheek to her father's heart. It was such a big, strong heart, it still loved her even when she made a bad mistake. It was such a big, strong heart, it felt like it was beating inside her, too.

In this life, sometimes words help you feel better. And sometimes, you don't need them at all.

21
Fixing Things

When Mom heard about the big bike chase, she was not what you'd call happy.

"That was foolish and dangerous," she said. "Anything could have happened!"

"But it didn't. And we got the Cobra back."

"That is not the point."

Mothers certainly had a different way of looking at things.

Mom paced up and down in her blue suede booties. Cody and Wyatt traded nervous looks. What would their consequences be? No screen time for a month? No candy till they went to college?

At last Mom paused. She took two calming breaths.

"You two stuck together," she said. "And you stuck up for what is right. In this family, those are important rules."

What was going on? Were they in trouble or not?

Mom shook her finger at them. "Never, ever do anything like that again," she said, just before she wrapped them both in a giant hug.

"Whew," said Cody as she and Wyatt walked out to the garage. "What just happened?"

Wyatt laughed. "I think Mom was saying that now and then, it's okay to bend the rules."

Cody imagined a rule doing a backbend. That made her laugh, too.

Dad was in the garage, examining the Cobra. He said they should take it to the bike shop, but Wyatt shook his head.

"It's my bike. I take responsibility for it. I watched some videos on the computer. I think I can fix it myself." He tapped Cody's head. "Plus, I have an assistant."

"So you do." Dad grinned. "A first-class assistant."

To fix a flat, you have to take off the tire, then remove the tube, then pump air inside to find the leak. Then you have to clean it, and make a patch, and make sure the patch sticks. Then you have to put it all back together. You have to pay attention to things called valve stems and tire beads. You need to use a special tool called a tire lever.

If you are thinking this takes patience, and your fingers will feel like frozen fish sticks, and a garage floor is not the world's most comfortable place, you are *correcto*.

If you are also thinking you'll feel proud and satisfied, *ding-ding!* You are right again.

Wyatt test-rode the Cobra up and down the driveway.

"Good as new!" he said.

Not really. The tire had a patch. The paint had a chip. But Wyatt didn't seem to mind. He seemed to like that bike even better than before.

Cody thought she knew why. He and the Cobra had gone through a lot together. Brand-new things are nice, all right. But things you get to know, things you spend time with, and take care of, and have adventures with — they are nice in a different way.

That made her remember Gremlin.

She tried to un-remember him.

If only you could fix everything with tools and patches.

Wyatt buckled on his new helmet. He strapped on his Hydration System.

"Tell *la madre* I went to see Payton."

"Okay."

Zoom. Her big brother was gone. Cody was all alone. Left in the dust.

But what do you know. Wyatt was doing a U-ey.

"I forgot something," he said.

What could it be? He had his toe clips.

"I forgot to say thanks for helping me. I couldn't have done it without you."

"You're welcome."

"You make a trusty sidekick, you know that?"

Zoom. He was gone again. But wait. Someone else was riding toward her. Fast. It was Molly on Wyatt's old bike. She skidded to a stop. She hooked the kickstand down. She looked at the bike with eyes of I-will-miss-you, then started to march away.

"Wait," called Cody.

Molly turned. She put her hands on her hips. "I brought it back!"

"I know. But, do you want to borrow it?"

Molly's eyebrows shot up like drawbridges.

"It may be old," said Cody, "but it's fast enough to catch a robber."

Overhead, the gray sky got a little crack and sun spilled out.

"For real?" said Molly.

"Wyatt won't mind."

"I'll give it back when you want."

"I know," Cody said. "You're trusty."

Molly's face did a quick-quick imitation of the sky. Before you could blink she was back on that bike.

"Out of me way!" she hollered.

22
Gongggg

Cody did not look forward to school on Monday.

The thought of seeing Pearl made her stomach spin like a washing machine.

The day was gray and dreary. Again. The clouds bulged like water balloons ready to burst. Cody's teeth chattered. What was the use of it being so cold if it didn't snow?

Pearl was already at their table. When Cody sat down, Pearl inched her chair as far away as possible.

Gongggg! Journal Time.

"It's free-choice day," Mr. Daniels said. "You can write whatever you want."

Gopal frowned and raised his hand. "What if you don't have anything to write about?"

"You have plenty to write about, Gopal," said Mr. Daniels. "Everyone does. Trust yourself."

"That makes zero sense," muttered Gopal.

"He's a rookie," whispered Pearl. "Just do what he says." With that, she picked up her perfectly sharpened pencil, bent over her journal, and got to work.

Spin-spin (Cody's stomach). *Tap-tap* (her pencil on her chin).

Pearl slid her journal across the table. Surprised, Cody read:

I have been thinking.

Cody gripped her pencil. She wrote:

Me too.

Pearl wrote:

About how angry you made me.

Oh. Cody sighed and pushed the journal back.

Pearl started writing again. Cody's stomach spun. Gopal muttered. At last, Pearl slid the journal back.

I thought, Cody went down the wrong road. Then I thought, So did you, Pearl. Cody's road was wronger. But it just goes to show. Everyone makes mistakes.

When Cody looked up, Pearl was holding an origami bird.

"It's for you. A dove, the symbol of peace. I'm sorry the wing got slimed. The babies did it."

Cody's heart grew a little feather of hope.

"Does this mean you're not mad anymore?" she asked.

"I was never mad. I was angry," Pearl said. "But not anymore."

Another feather.

"So do you want to be friends again?"

"Do you?"

"Do bears poop in the woods?"

Pearl giggled.

"Cody and Pearl, are you on task?" called Mr. Daniels.

Pearl put her hand over her rule-following mouth, but the giggles sneaked out between her fingers. By now, Cody's heart was covered in feathers. It flapped its wings.

Gongggg! That beautiful sound!

"Recess Time," said Mr. Daniels. "Don't forget hats and mittens. It's very cold out."

"My grandmother is coming for the holidays," said Pearl as they pulled on their jackets. "She'll want to see my endangered collection. Including Foxy." She looked at Cody. "I'm not sure what to do."

Flap-flap went Cody's heart.

"We could trade back," she said.

Pearl smiled. "That's exactly what I was thinking, twinner."

Cody's heart spread its wings and flew.

Instead of going outside, she ran back into the classroom. Mr. Daniels was flopped over in his chair.

He had chalk on his cheek. Being a rookie must really take it out of you.

Cody stood in front of his desk. The N-N gong was so close, her fingers got that dangerous itch. She scrunched her hands inside her pockets.

"You know what, Mr. Daniels?" she said. "You were right. Writing can help you figure things out."

Her teacher sat up straighter. He smiled.

"Thank you for sharing that, Cody."

"And guess what else? We got the Cobra back."

His smile faded. "Oh. You did?" He smoothed his cowlick. *Sproing!*

"And you know what else? Your cowlick reminds me of a Madagascar hissing cockroach."

Back came his smile. "From you, Cody, I'll take that as a compliment."

Outside, a shout went up. They looked out the window and what do you know! It was starting to snow! Flakes drifted down like tiny, perfect stars. Soon, the air was dizzy with them. Everyone ran around, shouting and laughing and sticking out their tongues.

"I love snow," said Mr. Daniels.

"Me too," said Cody.

They stood side by side, loving the snow together. Then Mr. Daniels said something her ears could not believe.

"Cody, would you like to try my gong?"

"What?" she sputtered. "I mean, yes! But it's an N-N rule."

"It is," her teacher said. "And you've done a wonderful job obeying it, even though I've noticed how hard that is for you."

"It is! It's very hard!"

"Just one time," Mr. Daniels said.

Cody went up on her toes. She stretched her vertebrate spine. Outside the old gray day was turning white and sparkly. Inside, Cody was about to break a rule, but not really. Amazing and unpredictable, those were the words for this moment. Maybe for all the moments. For the whole world! Cody lifted the hammer. She could already feel the hushed, beautiful sound spreading through her, all the way from her fingers to her toes.

Gongggg!